BROKEN WINGS

SUHAS

 pencil

ISBN 978-93-5667-109-6
© SUHAS 2022
Published in India 2022 by Pencil

A brand of
One Point Six Technologies Pvt. Ltd.
123, Building J2, Shram Seva Premises,
Wadala Truck Terminal, Wadala (E)
Mumbai 400037, Maharashtra, INDIA
E connect@thepencilapp.com
W www.thepencilapp.com

Author biography

Born in 1961, in a remote village named Karuigachi, now under Tehatta Sub-Division in Nadia district, West Bengal, India. He was brought up at his parental house at Areadanga, under Kaligang P.S, under the same district, Nadia, West Bengal, India. He had his primary education at the village primary school and after passing the Madhyamik exams, he was admitted to I.T.I Berhampur, Murshidabad. When he was in the second year, getting a stipend, he joined as a trainee at Garden Ship Builders and Engineers Limited and happened to be permanent, but unfortunately, it didn't come to reality. Passing the NCTVT Exams. he joined as a Fitter at a private company. He worked there for several years, but it didn't suit him. Not only that, he wanted to continue his studies, so leaving the job, he returned to his native village after eight years. As he passed several years in Kolkata, he couldn't adjust to the village atmosphere as he was a reformed man, besides, the economic conditions of the family deteriorated severely. At that time he started private tuition in the nearest town Mira Bazar, Plassey, Nadia. Gradually, the number of students increased, and he resumed his study. He got admitted to Krishnanagar Collegiate School. After passing the Higher Secondary Exams. He got admitted to Krishnanagar Govt. College and passed the B. A Exams. When he was a college student and going through an extreme financial crunch, he started writing short stories and poems to keep peace of mind. Some of his poems and short stories were published in magazines like Yuba Darpan, Dinanta, etc., from Kolkata, and during that time, the economic condition of his parents deteriorated drastically for the whimsicality of his father, who remained out of home and was less concerned about his family. Naturally, his father had to sell the property which his father inherited from his father. He started earning money through private tuition to make both ends meet, and at the same, time prepare himself for competitive Exams. To overcome poverty, he did not stop writing as it was his passion. Saving pennies one by one he managed to get his first book named "Thikanar Khonje"(In Search of an Address) published in 1989 by "Padma Ganga Publishers," Kolkata, but it did not find any success.

In the meantime, fortune smiled upon him, and got Govt. Service under West Bengal Govt. Though he had to pass most of the day at the office, it could not dampen his spirit to write. In the year 2009, his second book named Jalchobir Rupkathara was published by the reputed "Ekush Shatak Publication", Kolkata.

However, though his passion for writing remained in his heart, he had to stop it for several years for the education of his daughter and the load of office work, but he completed his M.A. in English through a correspondence course and again started writing novels in 2019 onwards. During this period he completed another novel, but it was yet to be published. This is his debut novel in English, named "Broken Wings."

CONTENTS

RIMI.. 9

Foreword

In our society, we come across so many men, women, and children in different conditions who suffer from many problems in many ways. Some of them suffer from hunger, some from social taboos and rituals. I get inspiration from them to write. I find it my bounden duty to express their situation through my writing to draw the attention of my readers who, I think, are the best medium to bring the situations to light. Some may ask why I write. I would like to say, "I write because I must."

So many incidents take place every day in our society, some of them are published in newspapers or broadcast through several media houses, but there are so many that remain behind the curtain.

Since my childhood, I have been noticing so many injustices are being done to the weaker section of society in many ways. Especially, women suffer the most, both mentally and physically. Even I saw my mother assaulted by my father, with a little fault of hers. Naturally, I was determined to write about the injustices of those suffering women. Besides, in our daily life, we interact with so many people and learn about various pathetic incidents from them. So I decided to write about those hapless people (men and women) to express my thought to my readers through my writings. Not only that, I have a passion for writing, and I can't stop it, as I have earlier told In this novel. I have depicted the characters from several strata of society and tried to express their joys and sorrows who live a simple life, who have minimal want and ambition, being born into a middle-class family how they sacrifice their love, desire, and long cherished dreams and how that minimum hope and aspiration remain unfulfilled.

I have tried my best to express my thought through this novel. Not only that, but I am optimistic that my readers will go through the book and inspire me to write more novels in the future.

Author

Acknowledgements

All the characters, incidents, and places mentioned in the novel are fictitious, if there is any resemblance to any living or dead, that is merely a coincidence.

Author

RIMI

Lying in bed, 1 heard the whistle of the last train for the night. It gives two whistles, one, when arrives at the station and the other, when leaves the station. Rivu, my elder brother, comes home by this train every month, but this time He didn't come home for the last three months. However, he rings me or my mother off and on. Whenever he rings me, he tells me that he is busy with his work, and sometimes if his mood remains fine, he talks about his friends, specifically, Vinita, his classmate, as well as a close friend.

Though I know that he is not coming tonight, 1 lent an ear to the gate. I could hear the sound of the passing vehicles and even the flickering of the light of them as our house stands by the road that had run from the station to the end of the village. The sound of the vehicles stopped after some time as the passengers come by this train are few. I heard the whistle too, and the rattling sounds of the wheels on the rails, and gradually the sound of the wheels died down.

I looked at the sky through the window. The crescent moon was hanging out on the western side of the sky and the stars were twinkling in the sky so far as my sight could go.

I tried to close my eyes but couldn't, so many thoughts came to my mind. I thought of Tuhin, my childhood companion. We were born and raised in the same village,- and studied in the same school. We used to go for a stroll to the station and had tea from the tea stall of Hamid's uncle in clay pots.

One afternoon, when we were returning from the station, it started drizzling along with the wind. We took shelter under the shade of a closed shop. The shade of the shop was so narrow that we were getting wet. I noticed that Tuhin was trying to save me from the rain. Even he told me to come close to him but I hesitated. I looked at him and saw that he was looking at me strangely. His eyes got fixed on my breasts for a second and a strange feeling ran through me. I too looked at him and for the first time, 1 regarded him as a man. My childhood companion turned to me as my beloved. When the rain stopped, I felt ashamed to look at him. I started running. I heard him calling, but I didn't look back. Coming home, 1 went to my room and lay down on my bed.
I don't know when the sunset and evening engulfed the earth. I began to think about my behavior with Rathin. It's not that I have met with him for the first time. 1 met with him often, especially on Sundays and holidays, but I didn't think of him otherwise. It's not that he looked at me differently, even though he once looked at my breasts when we were waiting under the shade.

When I was absorbed in the thought 1 heard footsteps, 1 turned back and saw my mommy enter the room. Coming to my bed she said," Why not sleep? The night has advanced much."

"My mind is getting distracted. 1 don't know why."
"Did you go into an altercation with Tuhin?"
"No, mom, but ---"
"Certainly, you have quarreled with him, that's why he didn't come to meet with us for about a week. Will you tell me the truth, dear? She looked at me for a few seconds and added," I know that you love him. I'm sure of that."
I remained silent, for 1 had nothing to say. She ran her fingers through my hair. I don't know when I fell asleep.

When I woke up the next morning, it was late and a ray of the sun has fallen on my bed slant through my beside window. I lay on the bed for some time more and tried to think about the incident of the last afternoon because it was not that I met him for the first time. We walked together, had tea from the same cup, and even walked hand in hand, but I didn't find fault with him. So why did 1 behave in such a way? 1 rebuked me for my rude behavior with him. I was thinking about what he would think of me. I got ashamed of my conduct. When I would meet him next, I thought I would confess to my fault.
 I heard that my mother was talking with my father about household matters. I rubbed my eyes on the wrong side of my hands and went downstairs.
I looked for my mom but didn't find her. My father was sitting on the couch on the veranda and Mati's uncle, our all-time assistant sitting by him.
"Good morning, my dear, ", my father said.
" Good morning, dad." I went to the kitchen and saw my mother making tea. I sat down beside her. She looked at me and said, ", you are late today, are you alright?

"Yes, mama," I told her a lie, otherwise she will ask so many questions.

Having prepared tea, she put it in the kettle and told me to serve it to my father and Mati's uncle. I kept the kettle before Mati's uncle and gave him his cup of tea and the second to my father. Taking the cup from my hand, he said to me, "Don't you like to sit in your books?"

"Yes, Papa, l am going to read." Though I told him that I was going to read, my mind was unsettled.

There is a small garden in the courtyard which my grandfather made after he retired from service, as my grandmother died early from a cerebral attack. He felt lonely. For the first few months of his wife's death, he talked very little. He stopped going to the station side, which was his everyday habit. My father is very obedient to him and there is a distance of opinion between them, so my father talked when it's necessary.

There are various flower plants like Jinia, Rhododendron, jasmine, and many others. In the center of the courtyard, there is a round concrete bench around a China rose tree. I went and sat on the bench. Petals of the flowers were spreading around the bench. A few sparrows were twittering in the branches of the tree. I know that they will fly away from the tree in search of food and come back just before the evening.

When I was in a dilemma about whether l should go to Mimi's aunt or not, my mother came to me with two cups of tea on a tray. Keeping the tray on the beach, she said, "What's the matter with you? I see that you are silent since morning and have not taken your tea till now."

"Nothing, mom, nothing wrong with me. I tried to smile and I know that my appearance deceived me."

I don't know what she thought, but looking at me for a while, she handed me a cup and she took her own.

When we were having tea, Lila, our maidservant, entered and came to mother and gave no chance to my mother. She said," I am a bit late aunt, my younger son has caught a cold."

"Why didn't you tell me? I could have sent medicine for him."

"You need not worry about it. I went to the quack, and he has given me tablets and told me that he would be alright in a day."

"Go and take your tea from the kettle."

When Lila was gone, mother told me to go upstairs and sit down to my books.

While going upstairs l saw his father gossiping with Mati's uncle.

Going upstairs, l went to the eastern part of the veranda and stood there for a while looking at the road. I saw the people of the village walking towards the station. I know that some of them work as laborers in the field while others work under railway contractors, but I couldn't stand there for a long time as the sunlight fell on me and I felt hot.

I came to my room and sat down to my books unwillingly.

ASIMA

Rivu came two months ago and, during the period of his absence from home, he telephoned me only thrice. When he rang me last week l told him to come home because the health of his father is not going well. He assured me that he would come home in a week or two, but two months had already passed by and the third one is going on but he didn't come. I sometimes wonder how it's possible for him who once would not like to live in the city and frequently rang me for coming back home is now going to forget the village. You are born and brought up here, in this village. The trees and shrubs, the ponds, the station, everything are known to you. How can you forget all your memories? What have you got in the city that is more important than your parents, your sister? Not only that, here is your sister Rhima you love, and asks me about you whenever she visits our home. Has the artificial glamour attracted you more than your village? It seems to me that the skyscrapers, the shopping malls, and the sophisticated girls have made you forget your village.

I was so absorbed in my thoughts that I forgot that the day has advanced much. I looked for my daughter, forgetting that I have told her to go upstairs and sit down to her books.

Lila was cleaning the utensils under the tube well. I thought of going to her and instructing her on what she should do after the cleaning, but a lethality paralyzed me to walk and I kept sitting on the bench.

Having finished cleaning the utensils, Lila came to me to ask what vegetables she should prepare for lunch. I was not in the mood to talk with her about it, but until I tell her about the menus for lunch she can not start, so I instructed her what to do. She listened to it but instead of going to the kitchen, she sat down beside me and said, "Do you feel unwell, aunt?"

"No, not like that, but I feel indifference. l don't know why sometimes it happens to me. I don't know whether others feel like me.

You have got everything: a nice husband, a nice daughter, and a good son. What do you want more? Aren't they enough to make you happy? If l were you, I would not expect more than these."

I sat there for a few minutes after Lila had gone, then I got up and went to the bathroom and poured a few pails of water until I felt cold.

My mind settled after bathing. Changing the wet clothes, l went to the kitchen to see what Mati was doing and giving her instructions l looked for my husband for l couldn't find him on the veranda. I went to the gate and looked around but could see neither my husband nor Mati.

Coming from the gate, l went upstairs to look for Rhima. When I was walking along the corridor l heard her voice. She was reading loudly. I have told her many a time to read silently, but she would not listen to me. Nobody listens to me -not my husband, not my son and daughter. I sometimes think about leaving the house and going to ancestry and then only they may realize my needs, but I can't do that.

Hearing my footsteps, she stopped reading and looked at me. She came to me and took me to her room. She made me sit down on the bed while she, too, sat beside me. She held my face and turned it to her and said," you know that Tuhin and I have been born and raised in this village together since our childhood and didn't think of him as a man, but I don't know what happened to me yesterday when we had to stop under the shade of a closed shop as it was raining. Because of the wind l was getting wet from the rain and Tuhin held me back to protect me from the rain and a strange feeling ran through my body. I looked at him differently. I began to think of him as a man- not my childhood companion. Can you tell me why, mom?"

I realized that she has grown into a lady and her internal physical changes have taken place. She has gained womanhood. Now I know why she is so morbid since yesterday. She has fallen in love with Tuhin but she couldn't tell me that. I patted her back and said, "Hmm, I think you're in love with Tuhin, Am I right? There is nothing wrong with it - a child, whether a boy or girl, will adult one day. This is natural dear, it's the natural law of the universe."

I don't know, mom, but I think of him, not as my childhood companion but as a ----".

I am your mother, dear. Besides, 1 am much more experienced than you. I have felt it throughout my life, so don't worry, everything will be alright with time." Though I told her that everything would be alright, I know that it is not possible.

When I was a child 1 too thought that life is simple, and our relationship with others is simple, to pass the time with the boys, to play with them, and gossip with one another while sitting side by side but when I reached a stage of the adolescent from a child 1 realized that life is not so simple as 1 thought. I know how 1 became a woman from a girl. I got afraid to meet with boys of my age, and insecurity worked on me. I sat beside her for some time and came downstairs to supervise the breakfast. I went to the kitchen and saw Lila had already prepared breakfast for us. I asked her if she had seen Mati or my husband, but she replied in the negative. I advised her to call Rhima, and I went out to look for my husband. Going out of the main door 1 around and saw him coming towards home with Mati. When they came near me l said, "Where did you go? Do you know the time now? "

"No, why.?

Look at the sky, the sun is above our head, it's going to be noon and you didn't take breakfast till now. I have many works in my hand but I can't do them until the breakfast is over." Where did you go?"

I went to meet Paran to tell him to plow the land as it's the time spread the seeds of wheat and rye, otherwise, it will be late and the production will be less than normal.

I had nothing to say, so I entered the house, followed by them. I told Lila to serve breakfast to Mati and my husband. I went to the kitchen to prepare lunch. I told Lila to bring the dry wooden stalks when her breakfast is over. I too had my breakfast and put the kettle in the oven to prepare tea. If l don't take tea after breakfast, it seems to me that breakfast is incomplete. I asked Mati whether he would take a cup of tea and he told me that he would like to have a cup. So poured four cups of water into the kettle put two logs into the oven to enhance the fire. As the planks were dry, they caught fire in a moment. When the water started boiling, l put some tea leaves into the kettle and covered it with the lid. After a minute, l opened the lid of the left and strained it with a strainer.

In the meantime, Rhima came downstairs with the plate of breakfast and handed out it to Mati. She came to me to gossip, but I was not in the mood to gossip with her, for my hands were full of household work. I don't know what she thought about me, but she went to the garden. I could tell her to meet with Thin, but I didn't tell them willingly. I left it to her to decide. A deep sigh came out of my heart. Leaving the thought of Rhima I engaged myself in cooking lunch as it was getting late.

Rajmohon

Nowadays l don't find any interest in anything. Even a few years ago I could engage myself in many household works. I used to dig up the soil around the garden, watered the plants and then broomed the courtyard. I could spend a lot of time doing this. My wife often complains me about my idleness but I can't find any proper answer that may satisfy her. Sometimes I think about my father who was much more active than me even at the old age. I ask myself why I am getting so indifferent to family life? It's not my wife and children don't love me. I have spent all my energy and labour for the wellbeing of them. I have send Rivu to Kolkata for higher studies, offered my daughter school education too, but I didn't send her to Kolkata like her brother for two reasons- first, I thought that if I send her to Kolkata like her brother, my wife will be lonely as most of the time l spend outside home for several works and secondly, if they don't come back home (if both of them get job) we shall have none to look after us during our old age though Mati came to our house as a servant he became a member of the family within a few months for his loyalty and honesty but Mari can't be a substitute for a son . In spite of that, I heaved a sigh of relief to have a companion to talk about almost everything to spend my leisure time.

After having breakfast, l along with Mati went to meet Paran and tell him to plough and harrow the cultivable land properly, otherwise the crops would not grow well and the production will be less than the normal. Giving him advice, we were coming home. When we were a few meters away from home, l saw my wife standing before the gate. We hastened our pace and entered into the house, following my wife. She complained that she was getting late for preparing lunch as our breakfast was not over. I didn't say anything because I knew that the day had advanced much.

After breakfast, Mati left for the mango grove a mile away from home to see if there was any dry wood in the garden for the use of cooking. I kept sitting on a chair on the varanda for a while looking at the garden. Shrubs grew around it as the grass was not mowed for a few days. The rains have stopped, and the sky has become cloudless. It's the time to mow the yard as the autumn has started the grass will not grow well.

I came down from the varanda and took the sickle from Mati's room and came across the courtyard. Placing the sickle on the concrete slab, l sat on the slab to think where to start from.

I started from the side of the gate because the sun will be hotter with time and I had to take an umbrella. I can't work with an umbrella over my head as it slows down the pace of working. Not only that, it seems to be an obstacle to me. Of course I take it when I go outside on a summary day and a rainy day.

When I was mowing the grass with the sickle, a smell was coming out of the wet soil. The smell was entering into my nostrils, a peculiar smell-a smell of the soil and some other materials.I inhaled the smell for a few seconds, though I have been talking the smell since childhood it always seems new to me. The characteristics of nature remain the same throughout the ages which is a miracle to me. Wherever and whenever you go and dig up the soil you will feel the same smell of it. Earth never betrays man, it's human being who betrays nature with the help of his superior knowledge and experience.

I don't know when my hoe stopped and I came to reality when Mati,my most faithful companion drew my attention. He has a peculiar way to draw your attention. He seldom addresses anybody by anything but coughs willingly so that one can hear him. Now too he coughed behind me to draw my attention and I looked back. I saw him standing behind me with a bundle of dry branches on his left shoulder,drops of sweat gathered on his forehead and a few drops rolled down his cheek. I told him to keep the wood by the side of the wall along the road and bathe but he wouldn't listen to me. Putting the dry woods he came to me and snatched the hoe from my hand.

I had nothing to do but obey him as l know that he wouldn't listen to me. Sometimes I wonder how he works hard though he is on the wrong side of fifty. When he came to our house l couldn't think that he would come to be a blessing to our family.

While leaving the courtyard l told him to take rest for a while,oth otherwise he would fall ill.

Ji sahib,by saying that he went to the concrete bench and keeping the hoe on it he sat down and started preparing khaini.

As I sat down on the chair on the varanda. my wife saw me and going to the kitchen she brought me a glass of water. I don't know how it happens because whenever I want something she comes to me with that thing. Have women a sixth sense? If not so how do they know what I need! However,tak tak the glass of water from her l ask about my daughter because I didn't see her since morning. I drank the water and stretched out my hand to her. While taking the glass from me she told that she was upstairs. She went to the kitchen and l kept sitting there.

RIVU

I was standing on the varanda of my one room flat. It's raining outside. I looked at the sky. It could not be ascertained whether it's evening if you don't look at your watch as the sky was slate grey and the lights were on. Everything was bathing in the rain water- the trees and plants, the buildings, and even the street lights. This was the second spell of rain during the week. The passing vehicles were splashing water from their wheels. A man who was walking along the footpath spreading his umbrella over his got drenched by the splashing water of a passing car. The man looked at his clothes and then shouted some words in vain as the car had already passed by.

I looked at opposite side of the road. A few dogs were lying on the footpath under a big bakul tree to save themselves from the rain water. Beyond the dogs a man in torn attire was sitting by the side of the wall of the tall building. There is a sun shade over his head and he was trying to save himself too from the rain water but the sun shade was too narrow to guard him. He had some food with him which he was devouring from a paper plate and looking around off and on. It may be for the dogs lying nearby. I turned my eyes from the footpath and taking out a cigarette from my panjabi pocket I tried to light it with a match stick but it blew out for the wind. I had to spend three sticks to light the cigarette. Giving a long draw l exhaled the smoke and tried to make rings but due to the wind the smoke rings could not be formed.

Oidrila rang me in the afternoon when I was still lying on bed and asked me to meet her in the evening at about 7.30.P.M.and I thought to but looking outside I doubted whether I would be able to meet her as the sky was darkened and after a while it started raining and I had to give up the idea of meeting with her. I rang her back and told that it was not possible for me to meet her in such an inclement weather. She told me that she was getting ready for going out and come to my flat, though I requested her not to venture out in such a bad weather but she wouldn't listen to me and giving me no chance she cut off the phone.I went into the kitchen and switching on the iduction I prepared a cup of tea.Going to the wooden shelf I took out the can of biscuits and wnt to yhe dining table as there was no other table in my room. I had my tea with biscuits as there was nothing stored in my flat for the lack of a fridge. I sat there for a while smoking cigarttes. I dont knok whether it was for the rainy weather I felt an urge for going home. Generally I go home in a month or two but this time two months have already passed . Mother rang me a couple of dys ago and complained that I had forgettin them The glamour and artificial life have chrmed me .I no loner feel for them but it is not true.Rhima too complained that the city girls had devoured my head and I must have fallen in love with a city girl for which he had forgotten Bultidi who loves him since her childhood. I did not tell them tat I met her when I went home last time.

It's the day of the immersion of the deity manasha. Five or six deities of manasha and two viswakarma idols are worshipped in the village every year.Especially the viswakarma puja at the station complex is observer with much pomp and grandeor. the whole station area is decorated with grlands and flowers and chains made of colorfulpapers are hung in various ways which increases the beauty of the place.During our childhood days we bathed in the early morning and wearing new clothes used to go to the station and witnessed the whole puja process made by the brahmin. After the end of the puje he spread water from a copper veshel ovr our heads and then prosad was distributed among the people,including the children and then we would come back home.Bulti, with whom I had had an affair, touched a flower which she was given at th time of offering the flowers at the foot of God viswakarma touched on my forehead hiding from thr eyes of others and murmured something which I did not know and kept the flower in her hand though I dont know what she did with the flower. Her love for me is quite different than that of Oindrila.

When I was thinking about my childhood companion,my beloved,a knock was heard on my door.at my door and putting on a vest I went to the door and stood behind it to be confirm of the knock. At that moment another knock was heard and the voice of Oindrila. Hello, Bitan,opn the door ,I have got wet,dont make me stand here. I opened he door and she rushed into my room.She really got almost wet by the rain water. Her light pink kurti got stuck with her body in such a way that her breasts were prominently seen through her kurti.To see me looking at her she told," Why are you looking at me in such a way? Did not you see me before?

I smiled and told her," Yes, so many times but today you are looking different,that is why I am looking at you .She looked at me and smiled i a mischievous way.She kept her vanity bag upon the dining table and sat down on a chair.Looking around the room she said ," I have to change my cloths,have you got to put on." Yes,I have. I went to my wardrobe and took out a pajama and a full sleeve shirt which I use in some occasions.Going to her I handed over the clothes . She took the pajama and full sleee shirt and while going to the bathroom she cast a side glance at me as if she liked to tell that I was a coward, if ther was anyone else he would certainly take the opportunity to make love with her in that situation.

When she entered into the bathroom I came and sat on my bed. I didn't like her coming at my flat at that time of the day, especially when the weather was so wet and inclement. My mind was getting distracted from reality. I was entering into the world of fantasy. I got surprised to think that a few minutes ago I was thinking about my village and Vinita and her avid love for me but now I was transported into reality and I began to think about Oindrila; her pleasant disposition, her cordiality, her jolly smiling face and, above all, her desperateness to lead her life according to her will.

On one such a October afternoon just after the Durga puja we went to a bar- restaurant to spend some time there. As it's a walking distance from my flat I set out from there a bit late. Coming down the road l looked at the sky. The sun had already downed the western sky and the colour of the light became yellow which fell upon the sky scrappers. The shadows of the trees lengthened and a mild cold breeze was blowing from the north east side. Some of the hawkers who close their shops at noon were reopening them. The number of footpath walkers was less as the office hours were yet to close.

It took me more than ten minutes as I walked at a slower pace. Reaching before the bar I took a packet of cigarettes as I ran out of it. It's a feature of the city. Before almost each and every bar or restaurant or a coffee house there are cigarette shops. As I come here off and on and purchase cigarettes from him,he knows both of us,Vinita and me. When I was paying him for the cigarette he informed me that Vinita had already come, wasting no time I climbed up the stairs and standing before the gate I peeped into the hall to see where she was sitting. A cloud of smoke was coming out of the gate and I am sure that if anyone who is not accustomed to such environment would feel suffocated sitting in the hall. I entered into the hall and looked around the hall. After a few seconds I found her sitting at the far end corner to the south west. Most probably she was keeping an eye to the gate,so when our eyes met she raised her left hand.Walking through the tables I went to her and sat opposite to her.n

 You are late today. I was going to ring you up.

Yes, I replied.

 Two glasses of water were already placed on the table. I took one of them and drank half of the glass. I took out the cigarette packet along with the lighter and kept them on the table too. She shouted at the sheds but none of them heard her for the clattering noise of the customers. Then she went to one of them and ordered on her will. Coming back to her seat she told,"Would you like to go for a ride?

When? I asked staring at her.

Getting out from here.

But the it will get evening then

You know that the day has shortened.

So what? Are you afraid of going out after evening?

No,not that exactly, but the scenario changes with the fall of the night.

O.K. then,I will not force you to do so.

In the meantime a bearer came to our table with the snacks that Vinita ordered and placing the plates on the table he left. I looked at the plates. Each plate contained two pieces of butter sandwiches,a chicken pocora and a cup of coffee. I calculated the approximate price of the dishes quickly and comforted myself to think that I could pay the bill though I knew that Vinita would do it.

Before eating the sandwiches l took a sip of the coffee and lighted a cigarette.l don't know why it happens; whenever l have coffee or tea l feel an urge to smoke.l don't know whether it happens to everyone else.

Vinita was chewing the sandwich and taking sipping coffee after chewing every piece.

I looked at her and saw that her face was pale which was bright and smiling a few minutes ago.l knew that she was offended for my refusal to go for a ride. I could not tell her that the city is not safe for women at night. Sometimes they are getting raped in the pretext of giving lift, even when she is accompanied by a male partner.

She was eating silently bending down her face. I knew that she was hurt but l didn't like to take the risk. To console her I said," Don't misunderstand me. We may go for a ride another day." She told nothing in reply l was in two minds as l was unable to decide what to do. Throwing the end part of the cigarette 1 said," Alright, let's go" By saying that I stood up and got ready to leave the bar, and at that time she caught hold of my hand and said," Please,sit down. and when I sat down again she added,"I know that you don't love me, there are many more beautiful girls than me and some of them hang around you for your bright career."

Don't be silly, you should know that I love you,of it's not so 1 didn't allow you to go to my flat and pass time hour after hour. It seems to me that you are a poor judge of character. If you like you may go to my flat instead of going for a ride..Now she looked at me and a smile appeared on her face. Generlly I dont like to take her to my flat at night which casts a different spell on human beings.Our sensual instincts grow during the night,a most rigid man may slip from his ethical senses. A ll the untoward incidents occur during nghts but I had no other way to pacify her. So I finished my snacks as well as coffee . She too finished hers as she was eager to go to my flat.

Coming out of the bar we started waking along the foothpath in slow pace as the number of pedestrains increased to a great extent. The situation aggravated by the hawkers who spread their goods on the footpath. This is the characteristics of Kolkata,the populas city of the Indians.

The night had already spread its wings over the earth and in spite of the street lights there prevailed a shadowiness in the narrow lanes where there was no street lights or scantily lighted.

This part of the city is very old . Most of the houses were built of bricks but of a smaller than the present ones.Even some of the buidings have not been repaired for a long tie and the skeletons of the decaying bricks had come out .

When we reached near our flat we heard the sound of conch shells from nearby houses which reminded me of village.Even now when I go home I can hear the sound of the conch shells which is still customay to the village women.

The sound of the conch shells still now soothes my mind.

On most of the evenings when I get back from office I take a bread from a shop under my flat for two reasons,firstly, I come back from my office at about 8.P.M.which is a bit late,and ,seconly, I dont find any energy for cooking at night after tedious work at office. I just bake the bread and eat it with butter. I asked her whether she liked to cook for the night or buy some food. She told me that she didn't like to waste time,so handing over key of th flat to Niva I went to bakers shop a few meters away from the flat. I bought chicken Tanduri and when the service boy of the shop came to give the packet ,the owner of the shop looked at me and said," hello,sir,How are you? You did not come to my shop for a long time." I had to say something in reply,so I said ,actually I stay here alone you know,so ,in most of the nights I take bread and butter for dinner,so I dont need to come here. He glanced at me through the corner of his eyes and narrowing them he said," I saw you pass by my shop a few minutes ago with a lady,your friend I think." Yes ,she is,I said.I was not in a mood to talk any more, I paid him for the pacage ansd walked upto my flat.

There is a small variety store just under my flat from where you can have many necessary things like cigarette,betel leaf,match box,pens,,exercise books, even wine,though wine sold secretly lest the police can learn and cancel his licence. I bought a packet of from him and ntered inti the complex. Though there is lift I dont use it as my flat is on the first floor. The security at the gate greeted me with a smile as he always does and I returned him the smile. Crossing him I went to the stairs and started climbing up the stairs. I was tired enough to climb up the stairs at a walk. I stopped in the middle of it and stood up for a few seconds holding the side bar. The surface of the bar seemed to be rough. It was not painted for a number of years,so, naturally.it was covered with rust.

When my breathing became normal I resumed to climb up. Reaching the passage before the door I stood for a while and then knocked at the door. A few seconds passed but Vinita didn't open the door,I again but no reply came from inside the room. I was getting impatient getting no reply,so I knocked for the second time and more loudly. Now I heard the sound of footsteps and there was a click sound inside the door and the door opened. Did you fall asleep? I am sorry dear,I let on bed and fell asleep for a while, don't mind. I entered into the flat without giving her any chance to talk more.

Going inside l put my bag on my bed and the package on the dining table. She shut down the door sat down on the edge of the bed. Her legs were dangling from the bed. As I felt hot l increased the speed of the ceiling fan and sat beside her. A smell of a fragrance came to my nose. I don't know whether it has any intoxicating power but it cast a spell upon me. I told her to wait and went to the bathroom to refresh myself. Entering into the bathroom l put off my clothes and opening the shower stood under it. The cold water cooled both my body and mind. I kept standing there for a while and then wiped out the water with the napkin which was hanging from the hanger. Coming out of the bathroom l saw that Vinita was preparing the dinner on the dining table. I thought that as the night had advanced much she was anxious for going home after dinner. I combed my hair and putting on a vest went to her stood beside. She was so absorbed in preparing the dinner that she didn't notice me. Having prepared the dinner she turned back and about to fall upon me. None of us were prepared for that and, naturally.both of us got surprised and bewildered at the same time and I could not help hugging her. S told nothing but kept her head on my chest. I inhaled the fragnance coming from her body. The time seemed to be endless,became eternal moment in my life. She left her whole body weight on me and a sensual feeling ran through my spine, my body became hot,l was about to take her to my bed and make love with her but within seconds the face of Bulti appeared before me. She reminded me that I was going to do wrong. My tight entanglement slackened and I freed her from my clutches placing a kiss on her forehead. I told her that the night had advanced much and she should get ready, otherwise she would not get a taxi to go back home. We sat down to have our dinner which was already prepared by Vinita. We are silently as if there was nothing to say. Having finished the dinner she she said," Take care of yourself,I will meet you soon." Saying this she took her vanity bag and opening the door went out.

When Vinita was gone l cleaned up the table and kept the utensils in the basin. I took the cigarette packet from the bed and came to the varanda. I looked at the sky. The decaying moon was hanging on the western sky and its silvery light spread upon the earth. As the sky was clear, the twinkling stars could be seen in clusters. I forgot to light the cigarette as Bulti appeared before my minds eye again.

In our childhood days in the village we(Bulti and me) used to go to the riverside and sit on a concrete slab till the evening and during the new moon nights, When the crescent moon rose in the sky along with some stars we started counting them indicating our fingers to them, then when the last conch shell blew we set out for home. We walked side by side along the dusty road. On our return journey from the riverside we talked little, only looked at each other now and then.

During the summer vacation we used to go to the river and swim in the water for a long time. As the water of the river remains transparent, even under water a man could be seen from a meter, though hazy. We dipped into the water we used to open our eyes to see each other and tried to catch hands. We remained in the water until we got tired,then coming out of the water we lay on our backs on the sand and see the blue sky. Though some men and women saw us, they didn't tell anything as they thought us merely children. Sometimes we would forget about time and went home late. On those days I entered home secretly and go to mother to enquire about my father. As he was a disciplined man he didn't like that I get back home late,if I faced my father while entering home ordered mother not give me anything to eat at lunch which was my punishment. Restrictions were imposed on me for a couple of days but I got restless in the afternoon and tried to convince mother so she would allow me to go out, but in vain, she consoled me to abide by the order for my sake. I had to wait for a couple of days to go out of home.

I turned my eyes from the sky and looked down the street. The movement of vehicles diminished to a great extent, only a few cars were plying long the road.The shops on the opposit footpaht were closed for the night,only the mall ,which I could see diagonally from there was still open.S ome customers could still be seen coming out of the mall but the number was very few.

 Ilighted the cigarette and had a long draw . I exhaled the smoke through the nostrila and mouth. The thin smoke that came out from my lungs looked bluish which spread in the air.An old begger was walking along the opposite footpath,he had a rolled rad under his left arm.He was wearing a full aleeve shirt which and a suit which,it seemed to me ,was not cleaned for a long time and had a number of holes here and there on it,the condition of the shirt too was torn and dirty,so it was impossible to ascetain the original color of both of them. Once he looked at the sky raising his head to measure the the depth of the night. He walked away slowly trailing his legs a few stray dogs followed him. Finishing my cigarette I threw away the end part if it.It fell down on the footpath and burned to the end then went out.I came back to my room and closing the door of the varanda went to sleep.

BUTLI

 After taking my afternoon tea I was thinking what to do.Once I thought to go to meet Rhima but left the idea,because now-a-days whenever I go to their house aunt asks me whether Rivu telephoned me .They think that Rivu rings me often. Sometimes I think to tell " You are his mother,so why he will ring me when he does not ring you why do you expect that he will ring me?but cant tell it." It is true that I love him since my childhood days,though it was not love in the beginning ,I had only a fascination to him but with time he became my favourite man ,my beloved,believe me ,I did not know how became the most favourite man of my life.I tried to distance myself several times to think of our economic status,my hlf educated parents and our sicial posion.In spite of the backwardness I was proud of my parents for their honesty,their frankness and neivity,are not these the quqlities of a family? So I fell in love with Rivu.

It happened all of a sudden,even I did not know that something strange was going to happen.Still then I used to put on frocks ,I was eleven, a grown up child but in the eyes of the villgers I was grown up as the reumer goes on in most villages but my parents did not think so,I was till a child to them.

However, on one evening when we were coming back from the river side after a stroll along the dusty road,Rivu stumbled at a stone and fell to the ground and screamed and could not stand up. I was a few feet behind him ; I ran to him and saw blood was oozing out from his right toe. I got so afraid to the blood that I,too cried out in fear. I pressed my right thumb on the place from where the blood was coming out but it could not be stopped,so ,without thinking anything I tore a part of my scart and bound up the wound tightly with it hoping that it would stop bleeding but it did not and to aggravate my fear Rivu said," Bulti, I will die! I saw a snake pass before me ,dont know whether it has bitten me." I cried out loudly like a child and put my right hand on his mouth and said," Dont say so,you may not die in this way,if you die what will I do then?" Suddenly he pulled me up and pressed against his breast and ,immediately a strange feeling ran through my body,neither I could tell anything nor free myself from his clutches.I forgot about his wound then and though he freed me from his entangled hands I was got dumb but only stared at him quite for some time, and he too kept looking at me in a strange way. From that very moment I could not think him as a childhood companion,he appeared before as a different man,my beloved ,my sweetheart,my life and death. We did not talk to each other for the rst of the way but looked at each other off and on as if we had lost our voice anr our relationship glided in a different way which seemed to me more uncertain ,more difficult.

From that very evening l could not meet him frequently like before, something obstructed me to meet him,I felt shy when I met with him. I couldn't look at his eyes straight,my feminine instinct prevented me from looking at him directly. I started talking with him in the third person. When we sat on that very concrete slab l always tried to keep a safe distance from him. On one such evening while sitting on the slab he told that he was going to Kolkata for higher studies.Though l don't know whether he told me a lie or actually he was going to Kolkata. He also said that he didn't like to go to Kolkata leaving his parents, sister and her,by saying that he looked at me. I smiled and said," Bah! It's a good news, you will be highly educated, will get a job; get a beautiful girl to love with and get married to her. What is the use of remembering me,a rustic girl? I turned my face away from him as my eyes got filled with tears. I didn't like to show him that I felt sorry for him, couldn't tell him how l would live here without him. If he goes to Kolkata leaving the village I will have only Rhima but I can't share my thoughts with her about Rivu; after all he is her brother,so how can I tell her that I love her brother and feel for him. I can share everything with a person and she is my mother. Before entering the we stopped just a few yards away from his home. There is a Banyan tree opposite their house . We stood under the tree, the faint moonlight created zigzag shadows fell upon the ground. We stood still for a while under the shadow of the tree. The shadowiness created such a mysterious atmosphere that we forgot to talk as if the very atmosphere charmed us by it's magical power. I don't know how long we stood there speechless,then Rivu told that he was going by the afternoon train and he liked to see me at the station."Please take care of yourself and ring me whenever you like." I just nodded my head and l ran towards my home without looking back.

Thereafter many years have passed. He came home several times and met me but with time his conversation changed. He mostly told stories about his life in Kolkata, his friends; he told that he had to change his lifestyle to cope up with the modernity of the city.

Whenever he came home he sent Rhima to our house to inform me about his arrival,but of late when he came home last time he didn't send Rhima to our house though I heard from one of my friends about his arrival. I thought that he was busy with home work and forgot to send Rhima or he might think that he sent Rhima as usual and didn't ponder over it.

On one morning after two or three days after Rivu's arrival mother told me," I have heard that Rivu has come home a few days ago,every time when he came home he sent Rhima to our house but this time she didn't come here,Is anything wrong with your relationship?"

No, not lke that,may be that he has told Rhima but she is not finding time to come to our house. Though I told mother,but I doubted she believed me.

May be that she is not finding time but why are you not going to their house to meet him?

To console my mother I said,"Hm, I am thinking so."but I know that I can't go to their house, for, in such cases he may think that I am hankering to meet him, no,I can't do that. I may born poor but I have got my dignity and l can't loose it ,if he really loves me he will meet me. Consoling myself I engaged myself in household works. As it's November the day has become shorter than the summer days. I saw the day pass quickly before my eyes and afternoon came. After my lunch l lay on bed and fell asleep. When I woke up and looked out of the window l saw that the light of the sun had died down and it had turned reddish from yellow. Mother told me to go to meet Rhima but I know what she wanted to tell but I can't do that. You didn't teach me to bow down my head to anyone else whatever happens,so how can I go to their house whereas, neither he nor his sister came to our house. So I kept lying on bed looking out of the window and see how the passes away and the evening approaches. I hoped that Rhima must come today and tell me to go to their house. I kept lying lending an ear to the door.

When the rays of the sun died down and the evening spread it's wing on the earth, my mother came into my room with the evening burning insense stick,which is a Hindu ritual.It is believed that all the evil spirits go away as far as the smell of the insense spread in the air. As I did not switced on the light of the room,mother did it and finding me lying on bed asked," why are still lying in bed,cant you even show the evening light? Are you alright? Yes mamma,I am o.k.

Why are lying then? It is evening, one should not keep lying in bed now,get up,I am prepring tea.She left the room.

I got up going to the bathroom washed my hands and face and went to the ktichen. I sat down before the door of the kitchen. Hearing the sound of my feet she turned her head but said nothing.Her face turned red by the flame of the oven.SomIn those times I feel proud of my mother. she seems to be different,as if she is not in the rea world,as if she is living in another world.At that time she seems to be a most intelligent lady ,in spite of her limited education.In those times I feel proud of my mother."You are not going to meet Rhima ,I think." " Not mamma,I dont think so,if I go they may think the I am eager to meet Rivu,I cant make them think so."

 Having prepared tea she came out of the kitchen with two cups of tea she went to the varanda and I followed her. We drank tea together after a few days because most of the afternoons l remain absent from home and get back home just after evening. Naturally.the time to take tea gets over and mother don't like to prepare tea after that time. Then when father comes home from work tea is prepared for him and I too get the chance to have a cup of tea for the honour of my father.

After having a cup of tea he goes to the bathroom to refresh himself to shake off the exhaustion of the day's work. Putting on clean clothes he sits on the edge of the varanda and both me and my mother also sit by his side.

Then he tells us the whole story of the day, what he did,how his boss behaved with him or how he praised for his work and expressed his desire to give him higher incentive before the pujas etc. Thus an hour or two passed and I would go and sit down to my books and mother would go to the kitchen to prepare food for the night. We have dinner on the varanda sitting on cushions I can hear the shrill sounds of the crickets that come from the nearby bushes.

 As I didn't go out l sat down to my books on the varanda taking a lantern beside me, though electric poles have been erected but wires have not been hung,so the villagers lanterns at night for household works. It's heard that electricity will come before the Durga puja.

 Though I sat down to my books l couldn't concentrate to my study. I was thinking how a man can change so quickly! How can he forgot a girl like me whom he said to have loved! Which he told me several times,even in the evening before his departure he promised that he would never forget me,but I started realising during the last few years that he was trying to forget me. It seems to me that he has certainly has fallen in love with a city girl,of course he can love another girland there is no wrong in it,but what is the of playing hide and seek with me? He can tell me that but he does not and there lies my pain.There are so many girls more beautiful than me and it is natural that one will fall in love with one or another. Sometimes I think that I should meet him and tell you need not be ashamed of your new love ,your new plan to live with her,but dont feign with me ,I dont like that, I am not begging for your love,it should be sponteneous and wholehearted,but you dont have the courage to do so,you are a coward,a selfish mn by heart,but look at me.I can't even imagine to forget him in any circumstances and there lies the difference between you and me. The city has completely changed you,you have lost your simplicity,your feeling for the village folks,everything:now I can pity yoy but love you.

I dont know when father came home and refreshing himself sat on the varanda like all other days and it might be that I would not come to reality unless father called by my name.I closed my book and went to my father.

What's the matter with you? On other days I see you in the kitchen with your mother but you are inside the room, what are you doing Binu,(father doesn't use my original name, he always tells me Binu). Mother told before my answer, your daughter has become a good girl, she didn't go out this afternoon,l don't know why, but sat down to her books Is it true?

"Hm, I told her to go to meet Rhima as she didn't come to our house for a couple of days,it may be that she has fallen il or not finding time to come,so you should go to their house and see what is the matter with her. Besides, Rive ,too has come home but she didn't go, I don't know why."

"Binu,is anything wrong? Have you had any issues with Rhima? "

I know what father wanted to say, he willingly tell anything about Rivu.

Nothing is wrong father, you know that I go to their house frequently but no relationship lasts on one's will. It's true that I didn't go to their house but Rhima would have come, it's not that she doesn't come to our house, but this time I thought that she would come. Why l will go to their house every time when Rivu comes home?

"O.k,O.k. you need not think of that,if your mind doesn't consent you shouldn't do that."
 I sat beside them for a while and left the place to talk between themselves and I went to my room and putting off the light lay down in bed and tried to sleep.

Rhima

  I was reading a book sitting on a chair by the window and looking through it if I could see Bulti pass by as she sometimes go to the market in the morning. I didn't go to their house for a few days neither she came. She has her reason because if she comes to our house frequently , her acquaintances may think that she comes only for Rivu but it's not true. She is our childhood companion,both of me and Rivu. When we were children we used to walk and play together in the field, go to the riverside in the afternoon and see the sun setting in the western sky. We didn't think Rivu differently. We walked along the bank of the river hand in hand. We played hide and seek behind the saw trees that grew on the shore. Thus we grew up, sharing our joys and sorrow, but the our relationship took a new turn when we reached at the age of twelve, when a physical changes were taking place, when I could differentiate that a man and a woman is not the same,l can't meet with a man whenever I do like to and if I do so people will take it differently. So,as l reached at my womanhood I realized that the relationship between Rivu and Bulti took a different turn, that an affair of love has grown between them. Especially, Bulti became reserved and her visit to our house decreased. I was happy to think that an affair grew between them as 1 loved both of them. Besides, Bulti is intelligent and soft tempered,honest and truthful. I thought that,at least Bulti, the daughter of parents, would find some pleasure in her life.

 Since a relationship grew between themselves I stopped going out with them, 1 would show some lame excuse and avoided the company but As Rivu went to Kolkata leaving the village for higher studies 1 found enough time to spend with Bulti. On some afternoons we used to go to the riverside and sometimes towards the station. Generally I preferred to go to the station as I could sit down on the beach before the station building and from where I could see children playing football in the field by the side of the station road. More than that we would drink tea from the stall of Vijoy uncle in clay pots, though paper cups came into the market. I preferred clay pot as a smell would come out from the hot clay. A train arrived at the station during our stay and the platform became full of passengers and coolies. At that time the station campus would turn to be a busy plac but for a few minutes,then when the passengers went out of the station area,it would again become deserted., only a few collies and dogs loitered along the platform. We kept sitting there on the beach until the sun his behind the the trees and birds would fly back to their nests by flapping their tired wings On one such afternoon we were sitting on the same bench Bulti asked me," When will Rivuda come home?

I looked at her and said,"I don't know exactly but maybe next week as he told mother over telephone,then added,"Why? "Didn't Rivu ring you?"
"No"

"Don't tell a lie, I know madam, you are drinking water sinking into water."

"Really 1 don't know, why should I tell a lie, especially to you."

I looked at her through the corner of my eyes and saw that her face was pale,she became thinner than before. I felt for her ,poor Bulti!

I waited sitting at mt chair for a long time without reading a single of the book which remained open before me. I blamed Rivu, You have changed yourself going to Kolkata I know,I cant blame you for that, one may change to adjust himself with the circumstances,but how can you forget a girl whom ,you said have loved.You always asked about Bulti whenever you came home in the first few years of your stay in the city ,if I told that Bulti did not come to our house for a few daye you would send me to their house to take news of her and requested me to tell her to meet him,but now- a-days you dont do so ,even you do not ask about her. Even I can't be normal before for your negligence to Bulti,you are not doing justice to her,it is not desirable from you.

 As I could not concentrate to my study I got up and came out of the room to see what mother was doing. Though the time of breakfast was over she did not call me for it. I looked at the kitchen but could not see her,then I looked around the garden but she was not there.I went to the main gate and saw her standing at the gate.Nearing her I asked," What are you doing here"?

"Your father is going to the town to meet a doctor,his health is not going well."

"Why did not you tell me?I could have accompanied him."

 "You know your father,he will not take any one with

him,I told him to take me with he denied.Lets go,have your breakfast.

I came into the kitchen and had our breakfast together,while taking breakfast I asked mother whether Rivu was coming in a few days.

"He is coming tomorrow by the evening train."

"Really!"

"Hm, really."

"Oh! "after all he is coming,though after a long gap,still he is coming and there is my pleasure,but at that moment another thought came to my mind,the thought of Bulti and I asked mother whether he has asked anything about Bulti but mother kept silent and I got sure that he did not ask anything about her which disheartened me.In spite of that I was very in the prospect of his homecoming,after all he is my elder brother.

The next day, after lunch, I did not lie in bed lest I should fall asleep. I passed time by going through a storybook. I knew the time of the arrival of the train.I made a light make up ,as,after all I am going to the station and many gentlemen will get off the train,besides, a friend of Rivu may also come with him ,in that case he may be displeased to see an ordinary girl to be his sister.

Getting ready, I came out of my room and saw mother lying on a mat. Hearing the sound of my footsteps, she sat up ans said,"Where are you going? I told mother that I was going to the station to receive Rivu.

Are you going to take Bulti with you?

No,Rivu did not tell to tee her with me,now if I take her with me it may displease him and I can't do that,besides, why will Bulti go with me? She may be simple, but she has got her honor. Telling this, I went out of home and went down the road.

I started walking towards the station.As I was walking eastward, the rays of the afternoon sun fell on my back and I felt a bit hot but it was tolerable.The shadows of the trees lengthened, under the shade of a peepul tree a rickshaw puller fell asleep stretching his legs over the handles of it.The old bearded beggar whom I see whenever I go for a walk to the statin was sitting under a tree spreading his begging bowl before him.

When I reached the station, it was five past fifteen, and the train was scheduled to arrive at five twenty p.m.,so I sat on a bench of a tea stall before the station. The rickshaw pullers started reaching before the station for the passengers. A few years ago, the number was hardly ten to twelve, but now their number increased to a great extent with the increase of the passengers.When I was thinking to enter into the platform. The train blew a whistle and reached the station ,so I kept standing outside the gate so that I can find him out.

When the passengers started coming out of the station,I was looking at them and when most of the passengers came out, I saw Rivu come out of the gate. He was looking around,probably he was looking for me.

I went forward and called by his name,Rivu,here I am and I raised my hand so that he could see me.He was wearing a black jeans and a cream coloured T-shirt, his skin tone changed from tan to biscuit color.

Coming to me, he smiled, and I too did so. He had a trolley with him. I told him to hand over the trolly to me but he said that he would draw it himself. We went to the tea stall of --------uncle and had tea. There was a time when we three-Rivu,Bulti and I used to take tea whenever we would come to the station for a walk in the afternoon. Then when Rivu left coming with us, Bulti and I would come and took tea from the stall and nowadays Bulti too does not with me, now I alone come and take tea from the stall. Sometimes ----------uncle enquires of Bulti and I tell a lie that her parents do not allow her to come with me.

In the meantime, the sun had set, and the became dark,only a reddish tint could be seen on the western horizon. Some birds were seen to be flying in the sky leisurely.After having tea we started walking side by side after a few months.I was feeling happy to walk with him and thought that now he can be relied on,now my father may have relief and be proud of his son he has become a man and doing a respectable job but, at the same time, I thought that he would ask about Bulti, but he did not which disheartened me,I thought that i rather, while walking he mentioned the name of Oindrila, her amicable manners,her intelligence and about her family status.I stared at him to read his mind but I could not ascertain.I heard the name of the girl when he came home last time. I thought that it was casual, one may have girl friends and there is nothing wrong with it, one may have many girlfriends but only one would last till the end, but now I got sure that he has come closer to Oindrila than Bulti.

When we neared home,The street lights were turned on and the atmosphere took a utopian look. A mysterious shadowiness prevailed beyond the streetlights.I don't know whether this atmosphere is felt in the cities. I feel that these trees and plants,these meadows,the river and everything attached to this village has bound me, can't leave this village.

Reaching at the gate of our house Rivu pushed the door, but it was closed as was evening. Rivu called,"Mom,Iam Rivu mother".

In a few seconds, a click sound was heard, and the door opened.Rivu entered through the gate and hugged mother.Mother kissed on his cheek and went inside and I too, followed them, closing the door.

ASIMA

Rivu has come home after a long time,about two and a half months.He generally comes home every month but this time he is at home after two and half a month. Whenever I asked him when he was coming home he said that he was busy with his works,he was not finding time and I had nothing to say,I consoled myself by thinking that he must be busy with his office,but whenever he comes home he gossips with me and his sister most of the time.He talks about his office colleagues and friends but from the last time when he came home he talked about a girl,Oindrila or like that ,I can't remember the name,actually I don't like to remember the name as I have no interest about the girl. He is at home for three days but he did not want to learn anything about Bulti. When he was going out this afternoon I asked him, "Where are you going"?

"To the station,I did not go there for a long time."

"You may go to the river side and meet Bulti. She did not come to our house for a few days,may be she has fallen ill".

He looked at me in askance but did not say anything.

When Rivu went out of home I asked Rimi whether Rivu asked anything about Bulti but she replied in the negative. I was surprised to think of Rivus behaviour, it seemed to me that the girls with colourful dresses and vanity have made him blind ,he is now in the world of dreams,a simple village girl is drifting away from his mind. It should not have been so. You are born and brought up here, in this village, you have a spiritual bonding with the environment of the village. How have you forgotten this? Have you lost your aesthetic appeal to the village? How? For the glamour of the city? Have the girls with colourful costumes dazzling before your eyes? Doesn't this soil attracts you any more? Have you forgotten that in your childhood you used to walk from one place to another during the nights of Goddess Kali with Bulti and Rimi? Can a man forget his childhood memories like this? All these questions appeared in my mind but whom l will tell? He is now a city man, he will not understand my grief.

When I was thinking about all these things sitting on the varanda before the kitchen, Rimi came to me with an excuse that I should comb her hair. I asked her," Are you going to Bulti's house?

"I am thinking so but,at the same time I fear, she may be hurt as she wished that Rivu would meet her,or at least, he would send me to inform her that he has come home and wanted to meet her, but a few days have already passed since his arrival and I didn't go to her; naturally, she has reason enough to get hurt. I can't decide what to do.

" She has every reason to react,if I were in her I I too might react, but whether she react or not you should go and give the information of Rivu's arrival."

Though I was hesitant,I went out of home.The sun was down behind the tall trees and the orange rays have fallen on the ground filtering through leaves of the trees. A spring wind was blowing from south,some say that its time to fall in love,but none has fallen in love with me.

I read in a co-ed school as it was the only school in and around five kms.When I was a student of class eight a boy named Atin stared at me when there was no teacher in the class. He was thin but tall and his eyes were broad. In beginning I didnt pay heed to it but I followed him for some time whether he is attracted to me but could not come to any conclusion.One day when the school was over I was walking back home,he came and stood on my way.As I was expecting this I asked,"What?""Actually I want to tell you that I----.

"What actually you want to say,tell me I dont have time."

"Actually I love you, please don't tell anyone about this." and looked at me.

My face reddened, I was so bewildered that I found no words to say,as if someone chocked my throat. What does he say? If anyone heard what will he think? I couldn't speak for a few moments nor l could look at his eyes. After a minute or two l came to my self,l looked around and saw other students passing by me but I couldn't walk, my feet were stuck to the ground. I drank a gulp of water and started walking slowly along the dusty road.

I went to school as usual and hoped to see Atin in the class but to my surprise I saw that he was absent. I couldn't tell this to anyone else, even to Bulti. I didn't like to make him feel ashamed of. Though I didn't say anything to him in reply, for the first time a felt a suppressed joy.

I didn't see him at school for a week. I saw next Monday.He looked pale and thinner. I doubted that he had suffered from some illness. Though I looked at him for a number of times our eyes did not meet.I decided to meet him after the school hours.To speak the truth I could not concentrate to the classes,I was just waiting when the school hours would be over. As soon as bell rang for the days closure of the school hours I went out of the class quickly and waited for Atin a few yards away by the side of the road. Some of my classmates asked while passing by me," whom are you waiting for? Have you fallen in love with anybody?" but I did not give any answer.I didnt not what they thought of me,I dont care whatever one thinks of me,I am not obliged to anybody else.When I was thinking to walk , I saw Atin coming lazily,as if he lost his strenght. When he came before me I started walking side by side.He just stared at me once but did not say anything. I asked,"Why didnt you come to school last week?" Looking at me he smiled and said," I was down with fever."

Oh,I see,As I could not decide what I would say,I wanted to frank,so I said," You seem to be very weak,you should take care of your health."

We reached near his home and waving his hand he entered the house. I stood there for a few seconds and then resumed my journey to our home.

The time passed by and everything was going on as usual. I used to go to school regularly and had talks with Atin off and on but it related to household matters in such a way that nothing happened between us. Though I didnt give him any hint , I started liking him for his tenderness,his soft disposition and his wittyness, he too never referred to the matter of love making but a feeling of love towards him remained in my subconscious mind. I decided to tell him some day for I was trying to be sure of my love towards him but I could not imagine that I would not have any chance to tell him that I too love him, that my destiny will not allow me to tell my truth to him.

After the summer vacation when the school reopened and the students resumed going to school as usual,I hoped seeing Atin at schoolbut he was absent from school and my doubt that he might have gone somewhere came to be true. On the first da when I was going to school,I looked at the house of Atin and saw the bamboo gate at the entrance closed,I thought that they had gone to the house of some relatives and would be back soon,but when a month passed and they did not return I starteddoubting that something was wrong with them.

On one afternoon I went to thr side for a walk alone and when returning home I went to gate of their house and looked inside.I saw shrubs beagan sprout from te ground,creepers grew up along the bamboo gate,and moss spread on the ground too. I stood there for a while ,my eyes got filled with tears.I blamed myself for not telling the truth of my heart,everything has a timespan,you must do that within that period ,otherwise you may loose the opportunity and I did so.My heart started throbbing,I don't know how long I was standing there,I forgot about time and I might be standing there unless Jyoti uncle,a friend of my father would come to me and ask me what I was doing there.I said to him," Atin was not going to school for about a month, I have my book with him." I don't know what he thought but said," Dont you know that they have sold their house and left the village"?

I looked at Jyoti uncle to perceive whether he was telling the truth.but my face became pale as if someone has taken away my joy,my happiness,my peace of mind within a second.

Jyoti uncle said," Before selling the house Raicharan came to me , he said that he could not make both ends meet with his meagre income,besides, he was not getting work regularly, so he has decided to sell his house and go to his in-laws place who has assured him to manage a job for him.

I looked at him blankly,as if someone has taken away everything from me. After Jyoti uncle was gone I started weeping lest anyone should hear.Now I felt that the sun of my life had set down,I would have no light with me but it would not have been so if I expressed my heart to him. I asked mysely,why didn't I tell him that I love him too,but now everything is over ,I have thrown away my arrow and it will not come back to me.

I walked back home like a defeated warrior and only one question was haunting me," Why didnt I tell him that I love him,if I expressed my heart he might not leave the village,he could request his father not to leave the vilage.it might be that his father would listen to him and didn't leave the village, but I could not do that. ,It was my fault and I have to suffer for that. Trudging my legs, I reached home and opening the gate quietly. I looked around for mother and saw her in the kitchen and without going to her I straight went to my room and lay down. Lying on my belly, I wept so bitterly that my pillow got wet with my tears and don't know when I fell asleep. After sometime when I was half awake, I felt that mother was running her fingers through my hair but I did not move or sit up.I don't know whether she realised anything but asked politely," Why are lying in such an odd time? Is anything wrong? Did you meet Bulti? What did she say?

"No, I didn't go to meet Bulti,I went to the riverside."

"Are you not feeling well?"

"I am well." By saying this, I sat up and looking at her; I said,?Do you know Atin, along with his family, has left the village?" "Hm,your father told me a few days ago,but how did you know?

"Raicharan uncle told me."

 She glanced at me in askance,then added,"Do you feel for him?

"Anybody will feel for him, mom,he is so polite,so simple and, after-all, he was a talented student."

I don't know what she thought of me, but she raised my face with her right hand and said," If I am not wrong,you have fallen in love with Atin."

I kept silent, as I could not think of what to say.

"It's not unnatural.Every man and woman have to pass through this period,I too had to go through this phase of life.Human life is very complex,my dear.We can't do what we like to. There are so many turns and twists and the road to life is not straight,so don't think too much about it. It will hurt both your body and spirit.O.k, let's go, your father may come at any moment and will ask for tea."

I went to the kitchen with mother to forget the matter for the time being, but I was certain that it would not be possible for me to forget Atin throughout my life as he is my first love,how can I forget him? How can I love another man,no, I can't do that,rather I will remain unmarried,now-a-days so many women remain unmarried,there is nothing wrong with it. My father is a rational man,he will never give me pressure to get married.I don't think marriage is a must for a man or woman.I shall live with the memory of Atin ,my first man in life.

End

----

www.ingramcontent.com/pod-product-compliance
Lightning Source LLC
La Vergne TN
LVHW041439170726
843492LV00008B/2707